A Ringing
of Doorbells

by Thornton Wilder

*This play became available through the
research and editing of F.J. O'Neil,
of manuscripts in the Thornton Wilder Collection
at Yale University.*

A SAMUEL FRENCH ACTING EDITION

SAMUELFRENCH.COM

FOR PRODUCTION ENQUIRIES

UNITED STATES AND CANADA

Info@SamuelFrench.com

1-866-598-8449

AMATEUR RIGHTS IN THE UNITED KINGDOM

Plays@SamuelFrench-London.co.uk

020-7255-4302

Each title is subject to availability from Samuel French, depending upon country of performance. Please be aware that *A RINGING OF DOORBELLS* may not be licensed by Samuel French in your territory. Producers should contact the nearest Samuel French office or licensing partner to verify availability.

For all enquiries regarding Professional productions in the United Kingdom; Professional and Amateur productions throughout the rest of Europe; and motion picture, television, and other media rights, please contact Alan Brodie Representation (Victoria@AlanBrodie.com). Visit www.thorntonwilder.com/contact for details.

No one shall make any changes in this title for the purpose of production. No part of this book may be reproduced, stored in a retrieval system, or transmitted in any form, by any means, now known or yet to be invented, including mechanical, electronic, photocopying, recording, videotaping, or otherwise, without the prior written permission of the publisher. No one shall upload this title, or part of this title, to any social media websites.

MUSIC USE NOTE

Licensees are solely responsible for obtaining formal written permission from copyright owners to use copyrighted music in the performance of this play and are strongly cautioned to do so. If no such permission is obtained by the licensee, then the licensee must use only original music that the licensee owns and controls. Licensees are solely responsible and liable for all music clearances and shall indemnify the copyright owners of the play and their licensing agent, Samuel French, against any costs, expenses, losses and liabilities arising from the use of music by licensees. Please contact the appropriate music licensing authority in your territory for the rights to any incidental music.

IMPORTANT BILLING AND CREDIT REQUIREMENTS

All producers of *A RINGING OF DOORBELLS* must give credit to the author of the play in all programs distributed in connection with performances of the play, and in all instances in which the title of the play appears for the purposes of advertising, publicizing or otherwise exploiting the play and/ or a production. The name of the author must appear on a separate line on which no other name appears, immediately following the title and must appear in size of type not less than fifty percent of the size of the title type.

FOREWORD TO WILDER'S
A RINGING OF DOORBELLS

THE SIN OF ENVY

From the time he began dreaming up plays as a boy Thornton Wilder's vision of the theater transcended conventional boundaries, and to the end of his life his vision continually evolved and expanded. In 1956, he began work on what grew into an extravagantly ambitious project: two cycles of seven one-act plays based on the Deadly Sins and the Ages of Man. *A Ringing of Doorbells* represents "Envy" in Wilder's projected cycle on the Seven Deadly Sins.

In what would prove to be his final dramatic works, Wilder sought not only to explore the theatrical possibilities inherent in the Sins and Ages, but (as he phrased it in his private journal on Christmas Day 1960) to "offer each play in the series as representing, also, a different mode of playwriting: Grand Guignol, Chekhov, Noh play, etc., etc." In short, he envisioned nothing less than a *tour de force* of dramatic theme and form encapsulated in the economy and intensity of the one-act play.

Wilder did not complete the challenge he set for himself, but he came close. The surviving work enriches his dramatic legacy and deserves to be remembered as more than a footnote to his lifelong conviction (written soon after *Our Town* opened on Broadway in 1938): "The theater offers to imaginative narration its highest possibilities."

THE SINS AND AGES THEN AND NOW

A brief overview of the history of these plays will help readers place them in Wilder's career as a dramatist. Two Sins, *Bernice* (Pride) and *The Wreck on the 5:25* (Sloth), premiered in English at a special event in Berlin in 1957 (with Wilder performing in *Bernice*). For reasons that have never been clear, for he enjoyed the experience and felt that plays did well, he withdrew them. That same year a third Sin, *The Drunken Sisters* (Gluttony), written as the satyr play for Wilder's full length drama, *The Alcestiad*, proved successful in its premiere on the stage of Zürich's fabled Schauspielhaus.

Five years passed before the continuation of his ambitious scheme appeared on a stage in the United States. In January 1962, two new Ages (*Infancy* and *Childhood*) and a new Sin, *Someone From Assisi* (Lust), opened at Circle in the Square, then located off-Broadway on Bleecker Street, to the reported largest pre-opening advanced sale in that stage's then 11-year history. Billed as "Plays for Bleecker Street," the show of ran for 349 performances.

Then silence. After "Plays for Bleecker Street" closed, no more Sins or Ages appeared. When Thornton Wilder died in 1975 the public record of his 14-play scheme contained only four plays – two Ages (*Infancy* and *Childhood*) and two Sins (Lust and Gluttony).

Today, eleven of Wilder's Sins and Ages are available for production: a completed cycle of the seven Deadly Sins and four of seven Ages of Man. The source of the seven "new" plays is no secret. The missing pieces were found in Thornton Wilder's archives at Yale[1]. From this source, starting in 1995, his literary executor and family released the two plays withdrawn in 1957, *Cement Hands* (Avarice), and four additional titles (*Youth, The Rivers Under the Earth* [Middle Age][2], *A Ringing of Doorbells* [Envy] and *In Shakespeare and the Bible* [Wrath]) recovered and completed by the actor, director and friend of Wilder's, F.J. O'Neil. (Mr. O'Neil's valuable notes on the origin of each of these missing links follow the text of each play.)

The public reception of Thornton Wilder's long lost and new plays was gratifying. *The Wreck on the 5:25* was selected as one of the Best American Short Plays of 1994-95. In 1997, the Centenary of the playwright's birth, Kevin Kline starred in a premiere reading in New York of *Cement Hands*, and the works recovered by Mr. O'Neil served as the centerpieces of Actors Theatre of Louisville's 13th Annual Brown-Forman Classics in Context Festival.   Finally, as the capstone to the Centenary celebration, TCG Press in 1997 published the 11 Sins and Ages in Volume I of *The Collected Short Plays of Thornton Wilder.*

---

[1] No additional one-acts remain to be discovered in Thornton Wilder's archives at Yale.

[2] We believe Wilder intended *The Rivers Under the Earth* to represent Middle Age.

Wilder never followed conventional theatrical practice. As a young writer in his "Classic One Act Plays" of 1931, he swept away scenery and played provocative games with time and place. In the Sins and Ages, his farewell as a playwright, he is no less adventurous by way of settings, techniques, stage-craft and themes. One artistic trend of the day especially "fired his imagination" where these plays are concerned: his passionate belief in the value of the arena stage. "The boxed set play," he wrote in 1961, "encourages the anecdote…The unencumbered stage encourages the truth in everyone." Wilder felt so strongly that audiences should be seated as close to the actors as possible that Samuel French, for several years, was only permitted to license these plays to companies agreeing to perform them on a three-sided thrust or arena stage.

***

As part of its celebration of Wilder's one-act plays, Samuel French and the Wilder family take great pleasure in issuing new acting editions for the Sins and Ages long in print and, for the first time, acting editions of the seven new Wilder works. We invite those performing or teaching these plays to visit www.thorntonwilder.com for additional information.

– *Tappan Wilder,*
Literary Executor for Thornton Wilder

CHARACTERS

MRS. BEATTIE, sixty-five, crippled with arthritis

MRS. MCCULLUM, her housekeeper

MRS. KINKAID, a caller, forty-five

DAPHNE, Mrs. Kinkaid's daughter, eighteen

SETTING

The front room of Mrs. Beattie's small house in Mount Hope, Florida, circa 1939.

(**MRS. BEATTIE**, *sixty-five, crippled with arthritis, ill, of a bad color, but proud, stoical and every inch the "General's Widow," wheels herself carefully into the room in her invalid's chair. She comes to a halt beside her worktable and starts to spread out the material for her knitting. A ball of yarn falls to the ground. She eyes it resentfully. Presently, and with great precautions, she gets out of her chair, stoops over and retrieves the wool. She has just regained her seat in the chair when **MRS. MCCULLUM**, her housekeeper, can be heard offstage.)*

MRS. MCCULLUM. Mrs. Beattie, Mrs. Beattie! *(She puts her head in the door.)* I have the most extraordinary thing to tell you. I mean it's perfectly terrible. I'll put the groceries in the kitchen. *(She enters from the back, her hands full of parcels and herself breathless with excitement.)* – And they'll be here any minute! *(She comes to the front of the stage and peers through a window toward the right.)* They'll be coming down that street in a minute.

MRS. BEATTIE. Now, do catch your breath, Mrs. McCullum, and tell me calmly what you have to say.

MRS. MCCULLUM. I recognized them at once – both the mother and daughter. You won't believe what I have to tell you.

MRS. BEATTIE. *(calmly)* I think you'd better sit down.

MRS. MCCULLUM. But they'll be here any minute.

MRS. BEATTIE. Who'll be here?

MRS. MCCULLUM. These dreadful people…I know you won't want to see them. I'll just send them away.

MRS. BEATTIE. Did you get my medicine?

MRS. MCCULLUM. Yes, I did. – Here's the bottle. And here's the change. – There I was sitting in Mr. Goheny's drugstore – and *they* came in. – The medicine was two-forty; you gave me a ten-dollar bill. Here's…seven…sixty… The mother asked Mr. Goheny where Willow Street was…and asked him if Mrs. Beattie was in town!! And she asked him if Mrs. Brigham lived in Mount Hope, too. – You see, *that's* what she does; she goes to people's houses. – People that have been in the army. *High up* in the army.

MRS. BEATTIE. Did you cash my check?

MRS. MCCULLUM. *(fumbles in her handbag; brings out an envelope, which she gives to* **MRS. BEATTIE***)* Yes, I did. Here it is. Mr. Spottswood sends his regards and hopes that you are feeling better. – Oh, Mrs. Beattie, they're just common adventuresses. Don't see them.

MRS. BEATTIE. *(she verifies the contents of the envelope; then says with decision)* Mrs. McCullum, I don't like fluster. Now, you go over there and sit by the piano; and you don't say a word until I've counted to five. – Then you tell me what this is all about – starting from the beginning.

*(***MRS. MCCULLUM*** goes to the front of the stage and sits by an invisible piano, containing herself.* **MRS. BEATTIE***, calmly adjusting her knitting and starting a row, slowly counts to five.)*

One…two…breathe tranquilly, Mrs. McCullum… three…four…Where did you first see or know about this mother and daughter?

MRS. MCCULLUM. I do want to apologize, Mrs. Beattie, for being so excited, but *(again peering through the window)* I wanted you –

MRS. BEATTIE. Yes, Mrs. McCullum. You first met them – ?

MRS. MCCULLUM. When I was working for Mrs. Ferguson in Winter Park two years ago, they came to the door. She said that her husband had been in the army under General Ferguson…in Panama…no, in Hawaii…and what good friends they'd been. They don't beg. I mean they don't *seem* to beg. She says that the daughter has a beautiful voice and that she hasn't the money to train this girl's beautiful voice. And the girl gets up to sing and she faints.

MRS. BEATTIE. What?

MRS. MCCULLUM. Mrs. Beattie, the girl gets up as though she's about to sing, but she doesn't sing. She crumples up and falls on the floor. And the mother tells a whole story about how they're starving, and Mrs. Ferguson gave her two hundred dollars. But that's not all. The next day Mrs. Ogilvie called Mrs. Ferguson on the telephone and said that these two adventuresses had called at her house and the girl had fainted and she gave them one hundred dollars.

MRS. BEATTIE. *(knitting impassively)* Thank you. Did Mrs. Ferguson and Mrs. Ogilvie remember the names of these people?

MRS. MCCULLUM. No…but this mother seemed to know *all about* General Ferguson and General Ogilvie…They go everywhere and get money.

MRS. BEATTIE. Now be quiet and let me think a minute! *(pause)* Do you remember their name?

MRS. MCCULLUM. *(peering out the window)* No, I'm sorry I don't. But Mrs. Ferguson looked it up in the army register and it was there.

MRS. BEATTIE. How old is the girl?

MRS. MCCULLUM. Well, that's the funny part about it. I think she must be all of eighteen, *now*, but her mother dresses her up as though she were much younger – so that she'll be more pathetic when she faints.

MRS. BEATTIE. Does the mother look like a lady?

MRS. MCCULLUM. Yes…pretty much.

MRS. BEATTIE. *(her eyes on **MRS. MCCULLUM** with a sort of sardonic brooding)* Think of how full their lives must be! – Full…occupied!

MRS. MCCULLUM. *(with a start)* What? What's that you said, Mrs. Beattie? *Occupied!* – But what they're doing is immoral.

MRS. BEATTIE. I'd exchange places with them *like that*!

MRS. MCCULLUM. You're in one of those moods when I don't begin to understand a word you *say!* Anyway, you're not going to see them, are you?

MRS. BEATTIE. *(calmly)* Of course, I'm going to see them. – Mrs. McCullum, will you kindly get the hot water bottle for my knees?

MRS. MCCULLUM. I'll do that right now. But they'll be here in a minute. Won't you let me wheel you into your bedroom and bring you the bottle there?

MRS. BEATTIE. In the first place, I don't like to be wheeled anywhere. And whether they come at once or later, I'd like the hot water bottle now.

MRS. MCCULLUM. *(starting)* Yes, Mrs. Beattie.

MRS. BEATTIE. One minute: tell me about the girl. She has lots of spirit. – Is this daughter pretty?

MRS. MCCULLUM. Yes. – Yes, she is…and that reminds me: will you excuse, Mrs. Beattie, if I make a suggestion?

MRS. BEATTIE. Yes, indeed, what is it?

MRS. MCCULLUM. Excuse me…but I think I should prepare you. The daughter – it struck me at once – resembles, very much resembles, that…dear photograph on the piano. I mean I couldn't help noticing it. Will you let me take the photograph into your bedroom?

MRS. BEATTIE. *(impassive, only her eyes concentrated)* I see no need to change anything in this room, Mrs. McCullum.

MRS. MCCULLUM. I'll get the hot water bottle.

*(She goes out. Again **MRS. BEATTIE** painfully descends from the chair. She moves to the piano and gazes long at the photograph. Then she moves farther forward on the stage and turns her head down the street. She sees the couple. She stares at them fixedly and somberly. **MRS. MCCULLUM** enters with a hot water bottle.)*

MRS. MCCULLUM. Mrs. Beattie! You're up!

*(**MRS. BEATTIE** indicates with a gesture the couple up the street. **MRS. MCCULLUM** rushes to her side.)*

MRS. MCCULLUM. Yes! That's they. She has that sort of list in her hand she studies all the time. – Oh, let me send them away. They're just swindlers – common swindlers.

MRS. BEATTIE. Look! – She's studying her notes. – Yes, the girl – there is a resemblance…Isn't it strange…*(broodingly, with a touch of bitterness)* Young…and beautiful… occupied…

MRS. MCCULLUM. And wicked!

MRS. BEATTIE. *(dismissing this)* Oh!…Alive…*(starting to hobble off)* Alive and together…Bring them in here. Be very polite to them. Tell them I'm lying down. We'll make them wait a bit…If they don't have calling cards, get their names very carefully and bring them in to me…I'm going to receive them without my wheelchair.

MRS. MCCULLUM. Mrs. Beattie!

MRS. BEATTIE. And while they're waiting for me I'm going to ask you to bring some tea in to them.

MRS. MCCULLUM. *(looking out the window)* Oh! They're almost here!

MRS. BEATTIE. Alive and together – that's the point.

(She goes out.)

MRS. MCCULLUM. *(picking up her parcels and pushing the empty chair)* Why, Mrs. Beattie, you're better every day. You know you are.

(She is out.)

(The doorbell rings.)

(offstage) Mrs. Beattie? Yes. Will you come in, please? Who shall I say is calling?

*(Enter **MRS. KINKAID** and **DAPHNE**. **MRS. KINKAID** is about forty-five, simply and tastefully dressed. She was once very pretty, but is now pinched, tense and unhappy. **DAPHNE** is eighteen, dressed for sixteen; she is cool, arrogant and sullen. **MRS. KINKAID** selects a calling card from her handbag.)*

MRS. KINKAID. *(giving the card, without effusiveness)* Will you say Mrs. Kinkaid, the widow of Major George Kinkaid, a friend of General Beattie! And our daughter Daphne.

MRS. MCCULLUM. Mrs. Kin…kaid. Will you sit down, please. Mrs. Beattie is resting. I'll ask if she can see you.

MRS. KINKAID. Thank you.

MRS. MCCULLUM. There are some magazines here, if you wish to look at them.

MRS. KINKAID. Thank you.

*(***MRS. MCCULLUM*** goes out. The visitors sit very straight, scarcely turning their heads. Their eyes begin to appraise the room. When they speak, they move their lips as little as possible.)*

DAPHNE. *(after a considerable pause, contemptuously)* Just junk.

MRS. KINKAID. The cabinet's very good. *(They both gaze at it appraisingly.)* When you fall, fall that side.

DAPHNE. We won't get fifty dollars.

MRS. KINKAID. And do that sigh – that sort of groan you did in Orlando. You've been forgetting to do that lately. Daphne! You've forgotten to take your wristwatch off. Really, you're getting awfully careless lately.

*(***DAPHNE*** removes her wristwatch and puts it in her handbag. She rises stealthily and goes tiptoe to the back and listens. ***MRS. KINKAID*** has taken a piece of notepaper from her handbag, but watches ***DAPHNE****'s movements anxiously. As ***DAPHNE*** continues to listen, ***MRS. KINKAID*** applies herself to the notes in her hand, murmuring the words as though for memorization.)*

Manila, 1912 to 1913 with General Beattie and General Holabird…1907 to 1911…Do you remember Mrs. Holabird in West Palm Beach…The Presidio, 1910… Oh, dear…

DAPHNE. *(returning to her chair, cool)* Something's going to go wrong today.

MRS. KINKAID. *(deeply alarmed)* What do you mean, Daphne?

DAPHNE. I can always tell.

MRS. KINKAID. No. No…How can you tell?

DAPHNE. There's going to be all hell let loose. Like that time in Sarasota.

MRS. KINKAID. *(rising, passionately)* Then let's go. Let's go at once. If it's going to be like that, I can't stand it, I really can't.

DAPHNE. Sit down! Stop making a fool of yourself.

MRS. KINKAID. This is the last time. I cannot go on with this any longer.

DAPHNE. *(harshly)* Cork it, will you!

(**MRS. KINKAID** *sits down and sobs tonelessly into her handkerchief.*)

Of course, we've got to take risks. If we didn't take risks where'd we be? Do you want me to go back selling stockings?…I like risks…and if there's going to be trouble, I *like* it. I like talking back to these old witches…Pull yourself together and learn your stuff. *(pause)* Do you want to go back to that reception job in that hospital!?!

MRS. KINKAID. *(low, but intense)* Yes, I do, Daphne. Anything but this.

DAPHNE. Seventy a week! *(She again fixes her eyes on the cabinet.)* Yes, that's not bad. It could go with the table at Mrs. O'Hallohan's. And the rugs at the Krantzes.

MRS. KINKAID. West Point, twelve. West Point, twelve. – Daphne, if you do see there may be trouble, give me the signal. You get so furious you forget to give me the signals. – Schofield Barracks. General Wilkins…1909.

DAPHNE. *(eyebrows raised; she means she hears* **MRS. MCCULLUM** *coming)* Hickey!

(*Enter* **MRS. MCCULLUM** *carrying a tea tray.*)

MRS. MCCULLUM. Mrs. Beattie says she'll be happy to see you. She asked me to bring you some tea while you're waiting.

MRS. KINKAID. That's *very* kind, indeed. Isn't that kind of Mrs. Beattie, Daphne?

MRS. MCCULLUM. The marmalade's from our own oranges.

MRS. KINKAID. Imagine that? – I hope Mrs. Beattie is well. Mrs. Farnsborough spoke of her as…as convalescent.

MRS. MCCULLUM. Thank you, Mrs. Beattie's pretty well. *(silence)* Now, I think you have everything.

MRS. KINKAID. Indeed, yes. Thank you very much.

(**MRS. MCCULLUM** *goes out.* **MRS. KINKAID** *looks at her daughter's face anxiously.*)

DAPHNE. *(looking out into space, scarcely moving her lips)* Trouble!

MRS. KINKAID. *(almost trembling; pouring the tea)* The last time!

DAPHNE. Nonsense. Just do what you have to do and get it over.

MRS. KINKAID. You're very difficult, Daphne. You're cruel. – Well, there are only six more addresses in Florida… and that's *all.*

DAPHNE. *(blandly)* California's as full of them as blackberries.

MRS. KINKAID. We are *not* going to California.

(**DAPHNE** *goes over to take her cup. She kisses her mother.*)

DAPHNE. Poor dear mother! *(whispering)* You forget so easily: our house…our car…my wedding…

MRS. KINKAID. *(clasping her face)* Oh, I wish you were married, Daphne, and *this* were all over.

DAPHNE. Well, find me the *man,* dear. Do I ever meet any men?

MRS. KINKAID. Charles is such a nice young man.

DAPHNE. *(suddenly darkly irritated)* Are you *crazy?* Who's *he?* – Go back and study your notes. We've got to play our cards well today.

(**MRS. KINKAID** *'s eyes have fallen on the photograph on the piano.*)

MRS. KINKAID. Daphne! Do you see what I see?

DAPHNE. What?

MRS. KINKAID. That photograph, dear.

DAPHNE. What?

MRS. KINKAID. …The resemblance. It – it looks just like you.

DAPHNE. *(a casual glance)* No, it doesn't.

MRS. KINKAID. It's amazing. *(reopening her handbag)* I know who it is, too. *(reading some notes from a reference book)* "A daughter Lydia Westerveldt, born 1912, died 1930." She's beautiful. She hasn't your eyes, dear…but the shape and the hair: it's amazing.

(DAPHNE rises, stands before the photograph and gazes at it intently.)

DAPHNE. Lydia…general's daughter…

"Miss Beattie, may I have the next dance?"…

"I'm so sorry, Lieutenant, but I've promised the next dance to Colonel Randolph."

"My daughter's away at finishing school. I don't know when she'll be back. She's staying with friends all over New England."

(turning to her mother, sharply) She has a wedding ring on.

MRS. KINKAID. Do come and sit down, dear.

DAPHNE. *(to the photograph)* Of course, I don't like her. She had everything she wanted. She didn't know what it was to know *nobody*, to have to spend all your time among common vulgar people, to skimp –

MRS. KINKAID. Daphne!

DAPHNE. …and she didn't have to see her own mother insulted *(whirling about to face her mother)* like *you* were by Mrs. Smith.

MRS. KINKAID. Dear, I wasn't *insulted* –

DAPHNE. *(back at the photograph)* And you never knew what it was to be treated *just ghastly* by men, because you were poor; you didn't know anything. *(She spits at the picture.)* There! There!

MRS. KINKAID. *(has risen; keeping her voice)* Daphne, you stop that right now, and drink your tea. Sometimes I don't know what comes over you...

*(***DAPHNE*** returns, grand and somber, to her chair.)*

I never taught you to say things like that.

DAPHNE. *(airily)* I don't like the way she looks at me. *(rendered pleasurably light-headed by her outburst)* I feel better. I'm glad I talked to her.... Mother-mousie, we're going to be very successful today. I feel it in my bones...and tonight we're going to a movie, and *you know which one. (She hears a noise in the hall.)* Hickey!

*(Both compose themselves for the entrance of ***MRS. BEATTIE***. ***MRS. BEATTIE*** enters alone, walking with the greatest difficulty, but putting on a cordial smile.)*

MRS. BEATTIE. Mrs. Kinkaid, good afternoon. I am Mrs. Beattie. Don't get up, please.

MRS. KINKAID. *(rising)* Good afternoon, Mrs. Beattie. This is my daughter, Daphne.

MRS. BEATTIE. *(stopping and looking at her hard)* Good afternoon, Miss Kinkaid. Please sit down, both of you.

MRS. KINKAID. We want to thank you...for sending the tea. So kind.

MRS. BEATTIE. *(sitting down)* Mrs. McCullum tells me you knew my husband.

MRS. KINKAID. Mrs. Beattie...My husband, Major George Kinkaid, was in the Philippines at the same time as General Beattie. He was a lieutenant at that time – it was 1912 and 1913 – and probably had very little opportunity to meet the General, but he knew very well a number of the members of your husband's staff General Ferguson – then Colonel Ferguson; and Colonel Fosdick. *(***MRS. BEATTIE*** nods.)* I was not there at the time. I was very ill for a number of years and the doctors thought it inadvisable that I should make the trip to the Far East.

MRS. BEATTIE. Were you ever in the Far East?

MRS. KINKAID. No, I wasn't.

MRS. BEATTIE. *(to* **DAPHNE***)* And where were you born, Miss Kinkaid?

DAPHNE. *(slight pause)* In Philadelphia.

MRS. BEATTIE. *(turning back to* **MRS. KINKAID***)* I assume that there is something that you wish to see me about?

MRS. KINKAID. *(She makes a pause, and clutching her handbag begins to speak with earnest candor.)* There is, Mrs. Beattie – I am faced with a problem and I have called on you in the hope that you will give me some advice. My daughter, Daphne

*(***MRS. BEATTIE*** turns her eyes on* **DAPHNE.***)*

is endowed with a most unusual singing voice. Qualified musicians have told me that she has indeed an extraordinary voice. And in addition to that voice, a deeply musical nature. Professor Boncianiani of New York, who is recognized as one of the leading teachers, has predicted a great career for her. Perhaps, if you wish – a little later – I shall ask Daphne to sing for you. My problem is this – where will I find the means to cultivate her voice? So far I have been barely able to afford a certain amount of instruction…naturally, in a very modest way. *(She pauses.)*

MRS. BEATTIE. I see. You draw a pension, of course.

MRS. KINKAID. No, Mrs. Beattie, I do not.

(She takes a handkerchief from her handbag.) I do not. My husband's career in the army began most promisingly. I have here letters from his superior officers expressing the highest opinion of his work. But my husband had…a weakness. *(She touches the handkerchief to her nose.)* I find this very hard to say…he was intemperate…

MRS. BEATTIE. I beg your pardon?

MRS. KINKAID. Somehow…alone in the Far East…he took to drinking. And on one occasion…under the influence of alcohol…he forgot himself…He was, I believe, impertinent to a superior officer…

MRS. BEATTIE. To whom?

MRS. KINKAID. To General Foley.

(*Pause.* MRS. KINKAID *dries her eyes.*)

MRS. BEATTIE. How have you made your living, Mrs. Kinkaid?

MRS. KINKAID. For a while I assisted in a small dress shop in Miami Beach. Then I was a receptionist in a hotel.

MRS. BEATTIE. And now?

MRS. KINKAID. I have not come to you with any problem about our livelihood, Mrs. Beattie. I hope to be able to sustain ourselves; it is Daphne's career – her God – given voice – that I feel to be my responsibility. – I would like you to hear Daphne sing. She is able to accompany herself. (*She looks inquiringly at* MRS. BEATTIE *who remains silent.*) Daphne, do that French song.

(DAPHNE *has felt* MRS. BEATTIE*'s weighted glance.*)

DAPHNE. Mother, I don't feel like singing. I think we should thank Mrs. Beattie for the tea and go.

MRS. KINKAID. Do make an effort, Daphne. Mrs. Beattie has been so kind.

(DAPHNE *turns and looks at* MRS. BEATTIE *who meets her gaze.*)

DAPHNE. (*under her breath*) Mrs. Beattie has not asked me to sing.

MRS. BEATTIE. I should very much like to hear you sing, Miss Kinkaid.

DAPHNE. (*rising*) Very well, I will.

MRS. BEATTIE. (*distinctly*) It will not be necessary to faint.

MRS. KINKAID. (*bridling*) To faint!?

MRS. BEATTIE. It will not be necessary to faint. I have understood the problem. – Sit down, Miss Kinkaid. (*turning to* MRS. KINKAID, *with decision*) How much of what you have told me is true?

MRS. KINKAID. *(rising; with indignation)* I do not know what you mean. I have never been spoken to in such a way. Come with me, Daphne. *(to* **MRS. BEATTIE***)* Every word I have said is *true.*

*(***MRS. BEATTIE** *remains impassive, her eyes on* **DAPHNE***, who has not moved from where she stopped on her way to the piano.)*

MRS. BEATTIE. I shall not telephone the police unless you force me to.

MRS. KINKAID. *(about at the door)* The police! We have done nothing that concerns the police.

MRS. BEATTIE. They could ask you to give an account of the money you have received. – Have you an unusual voice, Miss Kinkaid?

DAPHNE. *(beginning with low contempt)* Oh, you can talk. You don't know what other people's lives are like. Our lives are just awful. You've got everything you want and you've always had everything you want. You don't know what it is for me to see my mother treated just like dirt by people she shouldn't even have to speak to.

MRS. KINKAID. Daphne! You know I've never complained –

DAPHNE. And everybody else has *cars…*and when they eat they eat things fit to eat. You don't know what it is to see your own mother –

*(***MRS. MCCULLUM** *has come to the door.)*

MRS. MCCULLUM. Mrs. Beattie, you remember what the doctor said… You're not to have any excitement. I must ask these ladies to go.

MRS. BEATTIE. *(raising her hand)* I wish to hear what they have to say.

MRS. KINKAID. *(comes forward as if there had been no interruption)* Daphne has not expressed our intention correctly. Daphne is a very imaginative child and is given to exaggeration. I have never made any complaint about our lives, as far as I am concerned; but you cannot know what it is, Mrs. Beattie, to bring up a refined and sensitive girl like Daphne…without money and without…any social situation. The only girls and young men we have any opportunity to meet are coarse, and vulgar…often unspeakably vulgar. Daphne's place is among ladies and gentlemen. I have spent sleepless nights – many sleepless nights – trying to find some way to better our situation.

DAPHNE. *(now going to the door)* Come, Mother, she doesn't know what we're talking about. She was born ignorant…and her daughter went from one dance to another dance…and her children would have the same thing. And what right did you have to a life like that? None at all. You were born into the right cradle. That's all you did to earn it.

MRS. BEATTIE. *(firmly but not sharply to* **DAPHNE***)* Have you a remarkable voice?

DAPHNE. No.

MRS. KINKAID. Daphne!

[*(***MRS. BEATTIE** *and* **DAPHNE** *look at one another.* **MRS. KINKAID** *and* **MRS. MCCULLUM** *are frozen where they stand.* **MRS. BEATTIE** *glances at* **MRS. KINKAID** *and then toward the antique cabinet on which stand the telephone and a writing kit with a pen holder and a checkbook. She moves carefully to the cabinet and pauses as if coming to an important decision.)*]

MRS. BEATTIE. [Alive and together…that's the point.]

[*(***MRS. BEATTIE** *picks up the pen and checkbook and turns back to face* **DAPHNE** *and* **MRS. KINKAID**, *as the lights fade)*]

End of Play

A NOTE ON THE TEXT

This play became available through the research and editing of F. J. O'Neil of manuscripts in the Thornton Wilder Collection at Yale University. In June 1957, Thornton Wilder wrote in his journal that *In Shakespeare and the Bible* and *A Ringing of Doorbells* were plays he could "terminate any day, but which will never be finished."[1] The author's manuscript of *A Ringing of Doorbells* ended abruptly with this exchange:

> **MRS. BEATTIE.** *(firmly but not sharply to* **DAPHNE***)* Have you a remarkable voice?
>
> **DAPHNE.** No.
>
> **MRS. KINKAID.** Daphne!
>
> **MRS. BEATTIE.**

Just how "terminated" is the play? The answer would appear to be: all but Mrs. Beattie's last line. After dinner one evening at his home in Hamden, Connecticut, Thornton Wilder read aloud to me a nearly complete draft of this play and spoke of his plan to bring the story to a logical, but unconventional, conclusion. Mrs. Beattie, as envious of the Kinkaids as they are of her, wants to help them in spite of their attempt to trick her. A fair solution then to the missing last line seemed to be a reprise of Mrs. Beattie's earlier line: "Alive and together...that's the point," as her summing up at the point of decision. The stage directions that I added are consistent with what appears to be Wilder's intention. Combining the antique cabinet and the telephone, both already established in the text, with a writing kit and checkbook, allows a moment of suspense as Mrs. Beattie moves toward the desk, and then a final tableau as she turns back to face the Kinkaids, checkbook in hand.

F. J. O'Neil
April, 1997

---

1. *The Journals of Thornton Wilder 1939-1961*, entry 749, page 266, selected and edited by Donald Gallup, Yale University Press 1985.

THORNTON WILDER (1897-1975) was an accomplished novelist and playwright whose works explore the connection between the commonplace and the cosmic dimensions of human experience. He won three Pulitzer Prizes: for his novel *The Bridge of San Luis Rey*, and two plays, *Our Town* and *The Skin of Our Teeth*. Wilder's farce, *The Matchmaker*, was adapted as the musical *Hello, Dolly!* He also enjoyed enormous success as a translator, adaptor, actor, librettist and lecturer/teacher. Wilder's many honors include the Gold Medal for Fiction from the American Academy of Arts and Letters and the Presidential Medal of Freedom. Penelope Niven's definitive biography, *Thornton Wilder: A Life*, was published in October 2012. For more information, please visit www.thorntonwilder.com.

Also by
Thornton Wilder...

The Alcestiad

The Beaux' Stratagem (with Ken Ludwig)

The Matchmaker

Our Town

The Skin of Our Teeth

Thornton Wilder One Act Series: The Ages of Man

Infancy

Childhood

Youth

The Rivers Under the Earth

Thornton Wilder One Act Series: Wilder's Classic One Acts

The Long Christmas Dinner

Queens of France

Pullman Car Hiawatha

Love and How to Cure It

Such Things Only Happen in Books

The Happy Journey to Trenton and Camden

Thornton Wilder One Act Series: The Seven Deadly Sins

The Drunken Sisters

Bernice

The Wreck on the 5:25

A Ringing of Doorbells

In Shakespeare and the Bible

Someone From Assisi

Cement Hands

Please visit our website **samuelfrench.com** for complete
descriptions and licensing information.

www.ingramcontent.com/pod-product-compliance
Lightning Source LLC
Chambersburg PA
CBHW070423120726
47909CB00005B/1777